Tort

written by Pam Holden
illustrated by Pauline Whimp

Hare and Tortoise had a quarrel about who could eat the vegetables in the farmer's field.
"Let's have a race to decide," said Hare.
Tortoise agreed. "We will race along the cabbage row tomorrow," he said. "The winner can have all the vegetables to eat whenever he likes. The loser will not be allowed to go to the farmer's field again."

Tortoise asked his family to help him win the race. "We will play a trick on Hare. He will think he is just racing against me, but there will really be three of us in the race. When we win, we will be able to have all the vegetables for ourselves without greedy Hare eating any," Tortoise told them.

Early the next morning, Tortoise's brother and sister plodded to the field, where they ate a delicious breakfast of cabbage leaves. Then Sister Tortoise went halfway along the row and hid herself behind the cabbages. Brother Tortoise walked on to the end of the row and hid under thick cabbage leaves.

When Hare arrived for the race, he didn't notice any other tortoises. Lots of animals came to see if Tortoise could win the race.
"Ready, set, go!" shouted Owl, and the race began, with Hare running quickly along the row of cabbages. Tortoise plodded as fast as he could on his short legs. As soon as Hare was out of sight, Tortoise turned back and hid near the starting line.

After a while, Hare looked back to see how far behind him Tortoise was, but he could not see him anywhere. He heard a voice call, "Here I am!" When he looked ahead, he saw Tortoise crawling along in front of him. Hare didn't know that Sister Tortoise had come out from her hiding place to trick him.
"How did you get there so quickly?" called Hare as he ran by.

He ran as fast as he could to reach the finish line at the end of the row of cabbages. But when he stopped running, he found Tortoise, munching on a cabbage leaf. Hare didn't know that it was really Brother Tortoise.

"That race was too short," grumbled Hare. "We will have to race again. I'm sure that I'm faster than you." Tortoise agreed to have another race, so they lined up while Parrot shouted, "Ready, set, go!" Hare ran quickly ahead, while Tortoise walked slowly.

When he was halfway along the row, Hare looked back to see where Tortoise was. He was surprised that he couldn't see Tortoise behind him, but he heard a voice ahead of him calling, "I am here!" Sister Tortoise had come out of her hiding place again.
"I don't understand how you can be so fast today," shouted Hare as he puffed past. Sister Tortoise crawled along, laughing to herself. As soon as Hare was out of sight, she hid under a large cabbage.

Tortoise was waiting at the end of the row again. Poor Hare was getting very tired, but he felt puzzled and disappointed. "How can you be faster than me?" he asked, puffing and panting. "We must need a longer race."
Tortoise agreed to race once more.

In the third race, Sister Tortoise played the same trick on Hare when he reached halfway and looked back to check. He ran on, getting more tired and slow. He was very disappointed to find Tortoise waiting happily at the finish line.

"You are the winner, Tortoise," said Hare. "I promise that I will not eat the vegetables in this field again." With a huge yawn, Hare hopped slowly home to sleep, while the tortoise family munched on cabbages.